THIS SUPER BOOK BELONGS TO

....

....

S

LADYBIRD BOOKS

UK | USA | Canada | Ireland | Australia | India | New Zealand | South Africa

Ladybird Books is part of the Penguin Random House group of companies
whose addresses can be found at global.penguinrandomhouse.com.

www.penguin.co.uk   www.puffin.co.uk   www.ladybird.co.uk

Penguin
Random House
UK

First published 2021
001

Text and illustrations copyright © Studio AKA limited, 2021
Adapted by Lauren Holowaty

Printed in China

The authorized representative in the EEA is Penguin Random House Ireland, Morrison Chambers,
32 Nassau Street, Dublin D02 YH68

A CIP catalogue record for this book is available from the British Library

ISBN: 978–1–405–94867–8

All correspondence to:
Ladybird Books
Penguin Random House Children's
One Embassy Gardens, 8 Viaduct Gardens, London SW11 7BW

SUPER DUGGEE

TAG

NORRIE

DUGGEE

BETTY   **ROLY**   **HAPPY**

Today, all the Squirrels are playing together in the clubhouse. All the Squirrels except Betty, that is . . . She is busy reading.

"What are you doing, Betty?" asks Norrie.
"I'm reading my comic," says Betty.
"What's it about?" asks Tag.

"Well," begins Betty, taking a big breath . . .

"It's called *Power Puppy*," says Betty. "By day, Power Puppy is a really cute puppy . . .

But at night, she's a really cute puppy that fights baddies and helps people!"

"Wow!" gasp the Squirrels.
"*And* she has special powers," says Betty.
"Like what?" asks Norrie.

"Like being *really* strong . . .

having *amazing* eyesight . . .

and a *super* sense of smell!"
says Betty.

"I wish we could be Super Squirrels," says Tag.
"Yeah!" everyone cheers.
"SUPER SQUIRRELS!" shouts Roly.
 Everyone giggles.

AH-WOOF!

Duggee dashes off to the laundry room.
There's a flash of light and a loud . . .

Duggee swishes his cape to one side in a superhero pose.
"Woof woof, woof woof!" says Duggee, pointing at a
badge on his chest.

"WOW!" gasps Betty, amazed. "The **Super Squirrel Badge!**"
"Woof!" Duggee nods proudly.

"I want to be a Super Squirrel!" says Tag.
"Yeah!" say Roly and Happy.
"You can't just *be* Super Squirrels," says Betty.
"Why?" ask the Squirrels, confused.

"You need a costume like Duggee —" Betty pulls her headband over her eyes — "and me!"
"Oooooh!" cry the Squirrels.

Happy runs off to the dressing-up box, and then comes back wearing a cape.

The rest of the Squirrels rummage through the dressing-up box too. They throw costumes everywhere, until they all find something superhero-like to wear.

"AND ME!" shouts Roly, with a colander on his head.

"I am . . . Brilliant Girl!" says Betty.

"And this is . . ." Betty nods at Tag. "You have to have a Super Squirrel name, Tag." "Oh, OK. Er," says Tag, thinking. "I am Super Tag!"

Norrie puts her arms up. "I'm Mega Mouse!"

"I'm Splash!" says Happy, jumping forward.

"What's your name, Roly?" asks Betty.
"Roly," says Roly.
"It has to be a *special* name, Roly," says Betty.

"Come on, Squirrel Squad!" says Brilliant Girl Betty.
"Let's go and do something SUPER!"
"Woof!" Duggee thinks that sounds super fun!

Super Duggee and the Super Squirrels head outside
in their super costumes.

QUACK!
QUACK!

"Did you hear that noise?" asks Betty. She follows the sound and finds . . .

"A duckling!" says Betty. "What's the matter, little duck?"
The duckling looks up at Betty.
"Quack quack!"
"Oh no, you've lost your mummy?" says Betty.
The little duckling sniffs and nods.

QUACK!
QUACK!

Betty picks her up.
"Don't worry – we'll
find her for you."

"Squirrel Squad assemble!" says Betty. "Little Duck
has lost her mummy."
"Quack!" says the little duckling.
"Ahhh," say the Squirrels.

"Mega Mouse!" says Betty. "Listen out for Little Duck's mummy with your super hearing."
Norrie listens carefully. "I can hear quacking," she says. "Over there!"

QUACK!
QUACK!

"Super Tag! Fly up and try to spot Little Duck's mummy!" says Betty.
Duggee picks up Tag.
"I see her!" Tag calls.
"By the pond!"
Betty turns to the rest of the Squirrels. "Let's go, Squirrel Squad!"

The Super Squirrels run off towards the pond.
"Oh no, that puddle is blocking our way," says Betty.
"Splash! Use your super splash to clear it."
"Splash! Splash! Splash! Splash! Splash!" says Happy.
"Good work, Splash!" says Betty.

SPLASH!
SPLASH!

Roly arrives at the pond first. "Over there!" he says.
"Oh no, they can't see us," says Betty. "Steven, it's
time to use your super shout!"

DUCKS!

Mummy Duck and the ducklings turn around.
"Quack quack, quack quack!"
"There's your mummy, Little Duck," says Betty.
The duckling happily swims off to her mummy.

QUACK!
QUACK!

"Awwww!" say the Squirrel Squad together.

Super work, Squirrel Squad!
Duggee is very proud of everyone.

Haven't the Squirrels done well today? They have definitely earned their **Super Squirrel Badges**.

"Hooray!" cheer the Super Squirrels.

"What's your superpower, Duggee?" asks Betty.
"Ah-woof . . ." says Duggee.